# ANNUAL

Published by
GRANDREAMS LIMITED
Jadwin House, 205/211 Kentish Town Road,
London, NW5 2JU.

Printed in Italy.

# CONTENTS

Peep! Peep! I am sure you all know who I am. My name is Thomas the Tank Engine. I've worked on The Fat Controller's railway for a long time with my friends and The Fat Controller thinks I'm a really useful engine. When I was told it was my turn to introduce the Annual this year, I felt very proud. Percy wanted to help too but, as you will see later, he has already been included in a book by a famous author and The Fat Controller said that too much fame could make Percy far too big for his buffers! You can read about lots of my other friends too. Skarloey gets scared when he hears noises at night, Edward has to be inventive to save the day and Rusty pays James back for being spiteful. Also all the engines help out on Christmas Eve to make the carol service a night to remember.

Packed with fun and games, I think you will enjoy your Thomas Annual very much. Annie and Clarabel, my faithful coaches, are waiting so I must go or I will be late to pick up my passengers.

Peep! Peep! Goodbye.

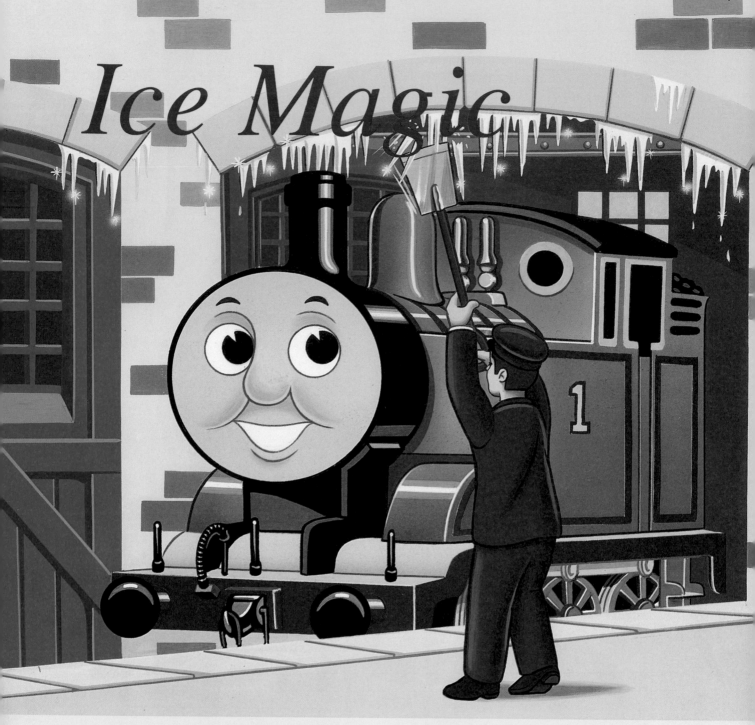

# Ice Magic

It was January on the Island of Sodor.

"I would like you to meet an important visitor," The Fat Controller told Thomas.

"This is Mr Bjork, an engineer from Lapland. He is on holiday here and will be helping us mend some signal boxes on the railway tomorrow. I would like you to take Mr Bjork around the island so he can start his work."

"Thank you Sir," said Thomas proudly.

The next morning it was so cold that icicles hung like a necklace from the front of the engine shed. Thomas' driver had to remove the icicles with a shovel. He 'bang-banged!' at the doors until they were free. Inside the shed, all the engines had been woken up by the noise.

Thomas was already awake and was steaming ready to go.

"You're in a hurry, what's the rush Thomas?" asked Gordon.

"I'm taking an important visitor around the Island of Sodor, goodbye."

"Pah," snorted Gordon. "Only important engines do that."

"Yes, stop showing off Thomas," puffed James.

Thomas was sorry the engines didn't believe him and he puffed sadly into the yard.

Outside, everything was frozen, including the engines' water tower. Without water, engines can't make steam and Thomas was worried.

"If I can't have a drink, I won't be able to go very far," he sighed.

Mr Bjork was on the platform. "I can help," he said.

He took an ice pick out of his bag and smashed through the layer of ice in the water tower. Thomas' tanks were soon filled and they set off. They worked hard all day and at last they reached the station by the reservoir.

"We'll drop Mr Bjork off at the

next station as The Fat Controller is waiting for him there," Driver told Thomas.

Suddenly Thomas noticed some ducks pecking at the frozen water on the reservoir.

"The birds need a drink too," said Thomas' driver.

"Perhaps Mr Bjork can help again," suggested Thomas.

And indeed he could. Every winter Lapland is white with snow and ice. Mr Bjork made a hole in the ice big enough for the ducks to drink through. Then he took a sharp chisel out of his tool bag and chipped away at the block of ice he had removed from the reservoir. In a few minutes he had made a beautiful model of Thomas.

"It's an ice sculpture," smiled Mr Bjork. "It's a present for you."

Thomas was very excited and his driver brought the sculpture into the cab so they could take it back to the yard. At the next station The Fat Controller was waiting. Mr Bjork said goodbye to Thomas and his driver

and Thomas puffed happily back to the yard. He was looking forward to showing the sculpture to the other engines.

"Where's the important visitor?" asked James.

Thomas briefly explained. "But he gave me a present, look!"

Thomas' driver stepped aside so that the engines could see the beautiful ice sculpture, but all that was left was a pool of water. The ice had melted in the warm cab and water trickled onto Thomas' footplate.

Thomas felt miserable.

"You came all this way to show us your leaky boiler," teased James.

"It was an ice sculpture," sighed Thomas. "Mr Bjork said so."

Next morning a wonderful surprise awaited Thomas. There stood Mr Bjork beside a beautiful ice sculpture of all the engines and The Fat Controller.

"We're sorry Thomas," said James. "Now we understand you had an important visitor. We would have believed you all along."

Can you help Thomas find his way through the maze?

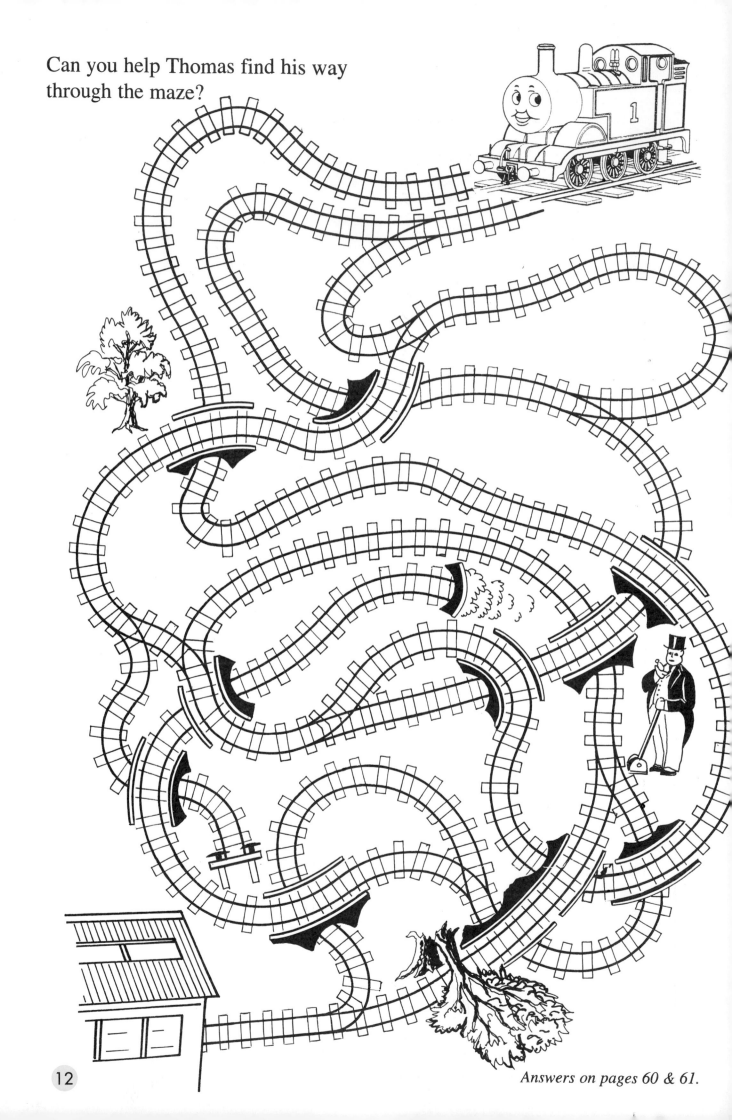

Answers on pages 60 & 61.

Look closely at these two pictures of Oliver and The Fat Controller.
Can you spot 8 differences between them?

*Answers on pages 60 & 61.*

James

# and Trevor

# Percy In Print

There was a lot of excitement in the station yard. The Fat Controller had just announced that a well known writer was coming to the railway to finish his book about famous steam engines and their journeys.

Gordon and Sir Handel were being cleaned for his arrival.

"I must look my best for my interview," boasted Gordon.

"Obviously only engines with titles will make an impression," steamed Sir Handel. "I'm a title, I'm a Sir!"

Percy brought Gordon's coaches. "What's an impression?" he asked.

Thomas explained that making an impression meant that you were important and everyone remembered you.

It was a bright Autumn morning when the writer sailed into the harbour from the mainland. Duncan was there to meet him with the Fat Controller. The Fat Controller agreed that the writer could ride in Duncan's cab. Duncan's nickname is rock 'n' roll and as usual he bounced and rocked all the way along the line. When they arrived at the station the writer didn't feel well at all and had to go and sit down in the Fat Controller's office.

"I certainly made an impression!" boasted Duncan to the other engines.

"Well, he'll certainly remember you," sniggered Gordon.

That afternoon, Gordon arrived at the station to take the writer along the mainline so he could take note of the journey for his book. Gordon was so full of steam that he raced along the line missing three stations.

"The journey was a complete blur," complained the writer. "The engine went too fast for me to see anything!"

Gordon took this as a compliment and boasted to the little engines.

Soon, Sir Handel arrived to take the writer back to the main station. The writer seemed relieved. "This looks like a sensible engine," he commented to the guard.

Sir Handel proudly let off steam as he waited by the platform. This blew the writer's manuscript everywhere. His papers were in a terrible muddle.

"I don't think the writer will forget me," huffed Sir Handel in the shed that night.

The next day a storm blew up and strong winds caused damage on the Island of Sodor. Trees fell on many of the lines and across some of

the roads. The writer was worried. He had to get his manuscript to the printers on the other side of the island. Today was the deadline, but the road was blocked. He telephoned The Fat Controller and explained.

"I know a route, it runs by the coast. We need Percy," replied The Fat Controller.

Percy was in the shed when his driver came to tell him the news. Percy was frightened by the strong winds, but he wanted to help. He puffed carefully along the windswept line. Sea spray splashed over the harbour walls and Percy tried to keep

steady while the wind whistled round his small wheels.

At last they arrived safely and the writer delivered his manuscript. He was very pleased with Percy and asked if he could take his photograph. Percy was delighted.

Many months later The Fat Controller came to the station yard with a big box of books. He gave copies to his staff. The contents were not what they expected. The writer was rather rude about engines like Duncan, Sir Handel and Gordon, but on the front page was a picture of Percy as a fine example of a little 6-wheel saddle-tank engine.

# Donald and Toad

| | | | | | | | | | | | | | |
|---|---|---|---|---|---|---|---|---|---|---|---|---|---|
| W | A | D | O | N | A | L | D | C | Y | O | L | R | R |
| H | L | E | F | R | R | R | P | S | B | T | A | E | A |
| I | H | F | U | A | O | G | O | K | N | L | C | L | L |
| S | E | D | N | I | V | T | H | G | L | E | W | O | O |
| T | N | H | N | L | E | W | I | O | N | H | E | C | C |
| L | R | E | E | W | R | S | R | A | E | E | L | L | L |
| E | I | N | L | A | T | T | G | E | B | N | L | A |
| P | E | R | C | Y | N | A | L | M | R | O | S | R |
| C | T | Y | H | O | B | E | R | T | I | E | W | A |
| O | T | L | C | S | E | Y | F | O | D | S | O | B |
| M | A | T | O | A | N | D | R | A | G | H | R | E |
| R | A | E | D | W | A | R | D | D | D | E | E | T | L |
| F | Y | H | M | E | C | B | I | L | L | D | H | F |

Can you find these words in the grid? They may be spelt forward backwards or diagonally.

**3 LETTERS**
BEN

**4 LETTERS**
SHED
TOAD
TOBY
BILL

**5 LETTERS**
HENRY
WHEEL
PERCY

**6 LETTERS**
BRIDGE
TREVOR
FUNNEL
BERTIE
EDWARD
SIGNAL
DONALD

**7 LETTERS**
WHISTLE
RAILWAY

**8 LETTERS**
CLARABEL

**9 LETTERS**
HENRIETTA

**10 LETTERS**
WELLSWORTH

**13 LETTERS**
FAT CONTROLLER

23

# Skarloey

Skarloey is a small red engine with a tall black funnel and a cheeky smile. He works with his friend Rheneas pulling passenger coaches. He is always eager to work and help his forgetful driver. Skarloey remembers the time he arrived at a station with cleaning brushes leaning against his boiler because his driver had forgotten to remove them. His driver even left two socks to dry on Skarloey's buffers once and poor Skarloey was teased by the other engines.

"Just look at his buffer mitts!" scoffed Sir Handel.

When it was Skarloey's turn to take passengers to the vicarage fete, he arrived rather late. Skarloey felt impatient. He was steamed up ready to go but his driver made him wait. He had lost his tea mug and was looking everywhere for it.

"Oh never mind Skarloey!" he said. "We musn't be late."

When they arrived at the vicarage, Skarloey felt hot and bothered because he had rushed to

# Gets A Scare!

make up time and his driver felt parched because he'd had no tea! Skarloey looked forward to lunchtime when he could sit in a siding and let off steam but things got worse! Driver's sandwiches went missing.

"I put them up there," he said to the guard, pointing towards the cab. "Drivers are like engines," he grumbled. "We need fuel to keep going too."

When they returned to the yard that night Skarloey was ready to rest in the shed. He waited outside while his driver opened the doors.

"Where's my torch?" his driver sighed.

Skarloey rolled into his dark shed without the friendly beam of light. The driver had lost his torch!

Skarloey's sleep was soon interrupted by loud rustling noises beneath him. He couldn't call to anyone because he had no steam so he shut his eyes tight and waited for daylight. Next morning, he told his driver.

"With all these noises and all my

belongings disappearing, something's wrong!" he said. "I'm calling The Fat Controller."

The Fat Controller confirmed that none of the driver's belongings had been handed in to lost property but said there had been reports of a burglary on the Island of Sodor so everyone had to be vigilant.

"I'll send a policeman right away," he said.

That night as Skarloey took a long, cool drink from the water tower, PC Penston arrived with his notebook.

"I'll watch over your shed all night," he told Skarloey's driver. "We'll soon solve this mystery."

Skarloey was shut up in his shed again but he felt less frightened now. BUT....no sooner had everything gone still than the rustling sounds began. Skarloey felt scared.

The next morning he told the policeman what he heard. Driver and PC Penston investigated the engine shed. They didn't find a thief but they

did discover a tea mug in the tool box.

"Oh! I put it there while I mended Skarloey's footplate!" the driver laughed. And a torch beside the telephone.

"Ah, I needed to see the phone book at night!" he recalled.

And a trail of sandwich crumbs, which they followed to a pile of leaves and paper shreds in the corner of the shed. Underneath was a sleeping hedgehog and her babies and the remains of the driver's sandwiches!

"Oh dear, I put my bag of sandwiches on the floor while I spoke with the fireman yesterday!" the driver said.

Skarloey didn't mind sharing his shed with a hedgehog and wasn't afraid anymore. It wasn't long before The Fat Controller arrived with a locker for Skarloey's driver to keep his belongings safe and a saucer of milk for Skarloey's hedgehog!

Gordon

and James

Bulgy is in a hurry to get to the station.
Can you help him find his way through the maze?

Answers on pages 60 & 61.

# Which two pictures of Diesel are identical?

A.

B.

C.

D.

E.

F.

*Answers on pages 60 & 61.*

# COMPETITION

*Win Really Useful Thomas the Tank Engine prizes in this free to enter competition!*

* Free membership to the fantastic Thomas the Tank Engine and Friends Club
* The new Thomas Cassette Recorder
* An audio tape of Thomas songs


* An exciting Thomas Action Watch
* A Thomas Christmas Collection video
* An audio tape of Thomas songs


* A Thomas Christmas Collection video

THE BIGGEST EVER
THOMAS
THE TANK ENGINE
& FRIENDS

CHRISTMAS
COLLECTION

One of the great prizes
you can win!

1. What number does Thomas have on the side of his body?
2. What are the names of the Scottish twin engines?
3. What colour is James?

# Edward Saves The Day

The school summer holidays had just begun on the Island of Sodor. Tomorrow was the day of the annual pony show - the Tidmouth Gymkhana. The Fat Controller's grandchildren, Stephen and Bridget, were making a special visit to join in the fun.

Later that day, The Fat Controller went to see Edward and his driver about the arrangements. "Tomorrow will be a very busy day and I need reliable engines to transport equipment for the gymkhana," he announced.

"Sir Handel and I will help," offered Edward kindly.

Early the next morning, Edward gave Sir Handel his instructions. But Sir Handel was flustered and didn't want to listen and take orders from anyone. He puffed off in a rush before Edward had finished explaining the arrangements.

"I know what to do! I know what to do!" Sir Handel complained. But he didn't. Instead of collecting show jumping poles from the riding school, as Edward had asked, he bustled straight past and onto the harbour station.

"Peep, Peep! I've come to pick up the things for the show," blustered Sir Handel.

"But I thought they were going to the mainland by boat," muttered the confused harbour manager.

Before long, the mysterious load was in Sir Handel's trucks and he bustled off to Tidmouth Station where the crates were unloaded and taken to the gymkhana field.

It wasn't long before The Fat Controller's telephone rang.

"What use are potted plants for show jumping?" shouted the organiser of the gymkhana.

The Fat Controller's telephone soon rang again.

"We understand our prize potted plants didn't arrive at the flower show on the mainland," sighed the

owner of the garden centre.

Edward heard that something was wrong and went to find Sir Handel.

"You've been very careless," said Edward to Sir Handel. "The Fat Controller will speak to you later but first we must sort out this muddle."

Sir Handel explained what he had done that morning and Edward soon worked it out.

"You didn't listen carefully," sighed Edward. "And the show jumping poles are still at the station near the riding school and the potted plants went to the gymkhana by mistake."

"Uh!" spluttered Sir Handel.

Sir Handel was sorry and wanted to help Edward sort it out. Together they came up with a plan. The gymkhana was to start at 2 o'clock so there was no time to collect the show jumping poles from the station. Edward told his driver about their plan and he told the gymkhana organiser who thought it could work, so everyone got busy.

After lunch, the children and their ponies arrived for the gymkhana. They were all amazed when they saw the colourful show

ring. Pretty potted plants stood in rows with garden rakes above them to make show jumps and pots of conifer bushes were laid out to play gymkhana games. The local newspaper came to take photographs and the day was a great success.

When it was over the owner of the garden centre presented the children with rosettes and prizes. Stephen, Bridget and the garden centre owner set up a stall to sell the plants. Everything was sold except for one bush which was eaten by a hungry pony!

The organiser of the gymkhana thanked The Fat Controller. "This has been a day to remember," he said.

The owner of the garden centre thanked him too. "I have sold more plants than I would have done at the flower show on the mainland!" he laughed.

Then The Fat Controller thanked Edward. "You Edward, have been a really useful engine, whereas you, Sir Handel, have been very careless."

"Yes Sir, I'm very sorry Sir," said Sir Handel, who this time listened very carefully indeed!

# Copy this picture of Skarloey into the grid below.

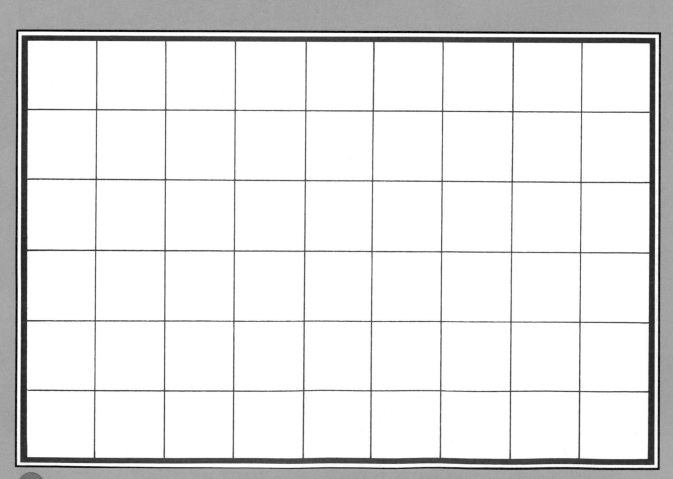

A picture for you to colour.

# Rusty's Revenge

Rusty is a busy little orange diesel who is always ready to help an engine in trouble and is liked by everyone. So when help was needed at the harbour, Rusty volunteered right away.

At the harbour things seemed busy. Trucks groaned and grumbled as they were loaded by a crane and trains shoved and shunted. In the middle of it all was an engine called James.

"I wanted help from the Express," called James rudely when he saw Rusty. "We need things done quickly round here. What use is a rusting old diesel?"

"I'm not rusting, I'm Rusty. My name comes from the colour of my paint which is rusty orange!" Rusty explained to James.

Rusty tried to ignore James. The little diesel soon organised the trucks and moved the load.

But James wouldn't stop teasing Rusty. "Don't shunt too hard or you might collapse!" peeped James. "Rusting engines soon get scrapped!"

Rusty felt fed up with James and so did the trucks. "He bumps and bangs us," they complained.

41

That afternoon, none of the trucks wanted to go with James to the windmill. There was a big consignment of flour to be collected but the trucks had been pushed around enough for one day. They made a big fuss at first, but Rusty told the trucks what to do and James was soon coupled up with no trouble.

"I know what's best for trucks," boasted James as he bumped out of the harbour yard. "See you at the scrapyard!" he called to Rusty as he went.

At the windmill, big sacks of flour were loaded carefully into the trucks. "Go steady now!" said the miller.

But James paid no attention. He wanted to get back to Rusty. As they approached the harbour, the trucks remembered what Rusty said and rushed forward. James's driver tried to slow down where the line bends,

but couldn't stop. "On, on, on!" they cried.

James was pushed right off the rails.

"Bump, bump, bump!" crashed the trucks behind him.

A big cloud of flour came down on everyone and completely covered poor James.

"Ha-ha-chooo!" he sneezed.

James felt very silly indeed when he saw Rusty puffing up the hill to help. With ropes and planks they soon pulled James back onto the line and returned to the yard.

The other engines thought it was a ghost train!

"Cinders and ashes," cried Percy.

"It's only James!" laughed Rusty. "I might be RUSTY but he's DUSTY!"

All the engines laughed, except James - who kept very quiet!

# Percy and The

# Fat Controller

Look closely at these two pictures of Trevor.
Can you spot 6 differences between them?

*Answers on pages 60 & 61.*

Join the dots to see what is blocking Thomas's path.

# Pipe Dreams

It was a cold January morning on the Island of Sodor. The Scottish engines, Donald, Douglas and Duncan, were working together in the station yard.

"Och, it's as chilly as the Scottish Highlands today!" shuddered Donald.

"Aye, it'll be snowing soon," agreed Duncan.

"Well, the hard work shunting the coaches should keep us warm," suggested Douglas when their drivers arrived.

"Come on lads," said Donald's driver. "Let's get this work finished before Burns Night."

Burns Night is a Scottish occasion which celebrates the life of a poet called Robert Burns. The Scottish engines hadn't heard his name for a long time and it made them feel homesick.

That day as they worked, they told the other engines about Scotland. When Percy brought empty trucks to the station, Douglas told him about the Scottish hills and

heather. When Stepney came to shunt the coaches, Duncan told him about the music that is made by playing the bagpipes and when Peter Sam arrived to help, Donald told him about the Loch Ness Monster who is supposed to live in the big lake.

"It's a Scottish legend," whispered Donald. "The monster lurks at the bottom of the loch, but sometimes it comes to the surface."

"Oh dear," shivered Peter Sam, who didn't like monsters at all.

"Is the Loch Ness monster as big as Gordon?" Peter Sam asked.

"Pah!" laughed Donald. "It's as big as a hundred Gordons!"

"Oh, no," squealed Peter Sam and rushed back to his shed to hide.

That evening The Fat Controller went to see Peter Sam. "I have an important job for you tonight," he said.

Peter Sam's fireman and driver soon arrived to get him ready. "Freezing fog is forecast. We'll need a lamp," said his driver.

Peter Sam puffed into the cold night with his carriages and trucks.

At the harbour they were loaded and Peter Sam set off along the branch line. The fog was very thick and he could barely see the tracks in front of him.

"Steady we go! Steady we go!" he puffed bravely to himself.

Soon they reached the lake and it looked very dark. Peter Sam remembered what Donald had told him about the Loch Ness monster. 'Supposing there's a monster here,' he thought.

He tried to pretend he was safe in his shed but an eerie noise made Peter Sam jump. He put on a spurt of speed to get away and heard three loud splashes in the water beside him. Peter Sam raced back to the yard as fast as his wheels would carry him.

Peter Sam arrived in such a rush that it woke the other engines.

"I, I saw it," he squealed to Donald.

"Saw what?" asked Donald.

"The M-monster," cried Peter Sam.

But, as Peter Sam's driver unloaded the trucks, the mystery was

solved. The train was full of things for the Burns Night party that was being held in the village hall. Inside the carriage were Scottish dancers wearing kilts and Rory McFearsome, The Fat Controller's colleague from the highland railway. One of the trucks was full of bagpipes.

"The wind must have blown through the pipes and made a moaning noise," said Peter Sam's driver. "It gave us a real scare," he laughed.

The other truck was full of small round objects. "These are called haggis," said Peter Sam's driver.

"You eat them on Burns Night. When you rushed off with such a start, some of the haggis rolled into the lake and made a splash."

Peter Sam was very glad to know there wasn't a monster in the lake after all.

At last came Burns Night and the engines had some surprise visitors. The Scottish dancers and pipers brought some delicious food from the Scottish highlands. The pipers played a tune especially for the Scottish engines and although they were homesick, they were very happy, just like everyone else.

# Rheneas and

# Skarloey

Can you find six fire buckets like this one in the picture?

Answers on pages 60 & 61.

54

Join the dots to see what is blocking Trevor's path.

# We Wish You A Merry Christmas!

Henry the green engine had a busy timetable but he didn't mind because it was Christmas time and his fireman Ted was singing carols in his cab. Each day, Ted practised a new carol and Henry enjoyed listening to them.

"Why are you always singing?" Henry asked Ted.

"I'm in the church choir," replied Ted. "We have to learn six carols in time for the carol service on Christmas Eve."

That night Henry told the other engines all about Christmas carols.

"Can you teach us to sing Henry?" peeped Percy excitedly.

"Don't be silly," huffed Gordon. "Engines can't sing!"

"But we can whistle," said Oliver.

This gave Henry an idea.

Next morning Ted came to light Henry's fire. Henry choked and spluttered on his coal and Ted didn't know why.

"What seems to be the trouble?" he asked Henry kindly.

"Er, nothing, I'm trying to sing," he replied shyly.

Ted laughed.

"I'm afraid engines can't sing," he sighed.

Henry thought for a moment, then he said, "But we can whistle!"

When they reached the harbour with their load Henry whistled extra loud.

"Poop! Poop! Hello Duck!" he called.

And Duck whistled back. Duck whistled to Oliver who whistled back to him. And Oliver whistled to James who whistled back to him. And Henry whistled to everyone. There was such a great deal of whistling to be heard.

The Fat Controller was working in his office and he soon came out.

"Please be quiet!" he ordered. "Engines should only whistle when approching stations or in an emergency," he added.

The engines worked quietly for the rest of the day, but Henry was disappointed.

"I would like to whistle carols," he told his fireman wistfully.

That night the engines had a visitor. Henry's fireman arrived with a songbook.

"You can help me learn my Christmas carols," he said.

Then he asked each engine to whistle so he could hear their sound. Gordon's whistle was loud and low, Percy's was high and shrill and Toby's bell added a nice Christmasy touch. He told each engine when to whistle and they learned to take turns. Soon they sounded like an engine orchestra!

The next day was Christmas Eve. It was time for the carol service. As Henry waited for his trucks to be

loaded, he saw his driver and Ted his fireman talking to the vicar. They all looked very concerned. The church organ had broken.

"Don't worry vicar," said Ted. "I have an idea."

That night the choir congregated at the church. Meanwhile the engines were helping Ted with his idea. They waited at the station beside the church and when Ted gave the signal they began to whistle all that they had practised the night before. The congregation were delighted with the harmony of the whistles that surrounded the church. Everyone finished with 'We Wish You A Merry Christmas' and the vicar was delighted.

On Christmas Day, The Fat Controller came to the station yard.

"You are really useful engines," he said. "Your whistles sounded splendid and the vicar's service was most certainly... er shall we say... an emergency."

# Answers

Page 12

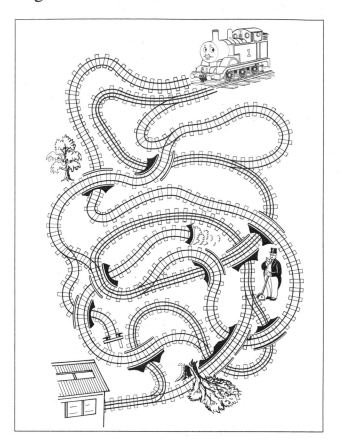

Page 13

Page 23

| W | A | D | O | N | A | L | D | C | Y | O | L | R |
|---|---|---|---|---|---|---|---|---|---|---|---|---|
| H | L | E | F | R | R | P | S | B | T | A | E | A |
| I | H | F | U | A | O | G | O | K | N | L | C | L |
| S | E | D | N | I | V | T | H | G | L | E | W | O |
| T | N | H | N | L | E | W | I | O | N | H | E | C |
| L | R | E | E | W | R | S | R | A | E | E | L | L |
| E | I | N | L | A | T | T | G | E | B | N | L | A |
| P | E | R | C | Y | N | A | L | M | R | O | S | R |
| C | T | Y | H | O | B | E | R | T | I | E | W | A |
| O | T | L | C | S | E | Y | F | O | D | S | O | B |
| M | A | T | O | A | N | D | R | A | G | H | R | E |
| R | A | E | D | W | A | R | D | D | E | E | T | L |
| F | Y | H | M | E | C | B | I | L | L | D | H | F |

**Page 30**

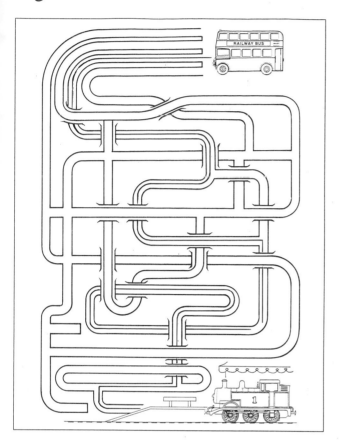

**Page 31: A and C are the same.**

**Page 46**

**Page 54**